My N is Miya

Written by Mio Debnam

Illustrated by Millie Liu

Collins

1 New Year's Day

It all started when Miya's gran called her Sadako.

It was New Year's Day and Miya had woken to the delicious smell of the Japanese ozoni soup that her family always ate for breakfast, on 1st January. Her stomach rumbled, and she ran to the kitchen. As she'd expected, Gran was standing in front of the stove wearing her favourite green apron. She was stirring a clear broth in which juicy bits of chicken floated.

Wrapping her arms around Gran's waist, Miya sang, "Akemashiteh omedetoh, Obaachan – Happy New Year, Grandma!"

Gran smiled and put her arms around Miya.

"Akemashiteh omedetoh!" she said, before nodding towards Miya's mum. "Eiko's cutting the carrot slices into flowers and preparing the mochi rice cakes for the ozoni. Can you prepare the spinach, Sadako?"

Miya pulled away. "What did you call me, Obaachan?"

Gran looked at Miya, her brow furrowed, then her expression cleared. "Sorry, I meant to say Miya. But I was thinking about how my sister, Sadako, and I used to help prepare for the New Year feast when we were young … and you looked so much like her that I got confused for a minute!"

Miya laughed, relieved. "Now, where's the spinach?"

Soon, the family were sitting in front of steaming bowls of ozoni. Kit, Miya's three-year-old brother fished out a piece of mochi, bit it and pulled, laughing as the sticky rice cake stretched out like cheese on a pizza.

Her dad, James, gulped down his second helping of the soup and patted his stomach in satisfaction. "Ahhh … So that's long life and good fortune guaranteed for another year, now," he joked.

"It's so good I'd eat it even if it wasn't supposed to be lucky," Mum laughed.

The morning passed quickly as they wrote resolutions and played games.

Then, as Mum and Gran prepared the New Year feast, Miya, Kit and Dad took their dog Toto for a walk across the heath.

"I'm a dragon!" yelled Kit, zooming around with steam pouring out of his mouth and nose as his warm breath hit the frosty air. Dad chased Kit, roaring and flapping his arms. Miya took out the sketchbook she'd got for Christmas and drew a quick cartoon of a chubby baby dragon in yellow wellies being chased by a scruffy white terrier and a dragon, wearing Dad's scarf and hat. She wrote "Best New Year's Day EVER!", then tucked her book away, and joined in the fun.

2 First day of term

The bell was ringing as Miya ran up the stairs of St Mark's Primary and into a group hug with her best friends, Jessie and Anika.

"Yay, I missed our J.A.M. sandwich hugs!" said Jess. She pointed to a flyer on the noticeboard. "Look at this!"

"Creative Clubs – Sign Up," Miya read.

"Year Six Theatre Club sounds super fun!" said Jess.

"Mum says we'll be working hard for our Standard Assessment Tests this year, so we'll need some fun!" said Ani.

Miya grinned. "Boo SATS, yay fun!"

"We're gonna be stars!" said Jess as they walked along, arm in arm. "How was your break?"

The memory of last Saturday's family gathering flashed through Miya's mind.

It'd been full of board games, giggling and fun. Just before dinner, they'd spent ages hunting for Gran's lost glasses. Miya's Uncle had howled with laughter when he'd eventually spotted them nestled in Gran's hair, but her parents hadn't even smiled.

Instead, an odd look had passed between them. Thinking about that look gave Miya a squirmy feeling, but she pushed the feeling away and said, "It was fun."

It was the first day of term, and she had exciting things to do with her friends. Miya wasn't going to let anything ruin it.

3 Theatre Club

Mr Kara, Miya's teacher, clapped and the hall fell silent.

"Year Sixes, let's recap. After-school creative clubs start next Thursday. Art Club will learn to draw manga, and Theatre Club will work on a musical I've written, based on *Alice in Wonderland*. If you sign up, you MUST make sure that you can be picked up at five."

"So, can you both join?" asked Jess.

"Yes," squealed Ani.

Miya did a little dance of excitement. "Mum's working part-time from next week, so she can pick me up."

"Yay!" said Jess, striking a pose. "Stardom, here we come!"

"I'm guessing you'll be in Theatre Club, Jessie?" Mr Kara laughed, walking by.

Jess nodded. "We all are!" she said.

"Oh!" said Mr Kara. "I thought Miya would do art, as she's always drawing."

Miya blushed. "I love art," she said, "but we decided it would be fun to do the play together."

"It's nice you're such good friends!" said Mr Kara.

They were assigned roles at the first meeting. Miya high-fived Ani. "Here's to the Queen, King and Knave of Hearts!"

She gave Jess a nudge. "Are you OK, Jess?"

Jess smiled, a tiny bit. "Yes," she said. "Though … I was hoping to be Alice. Maybe you shouldn't have said we wanted to be together, Miya."

"I didn't mean – " started Miya, when Ani butted in.

"Nah, it's 'cos Mr Kara wrote some awesome songs for the 'Heart Card Trio', and we're the three best singers!"

Jess took a deep breath and nodded. "Yeah, you're right," she said, but she didn't sound convinced.

The rest of the meeting flew by as they read through the scripts. Mr Kara sat at the piano and played a few of the chorus songs before it was time to go.

"I'll send videos of the songs to your parents. Please read the script and listen to the songs by next week, so we can start work!" he said.

The hallway filled with excited chatter as everyone poured out, and were picked up. Within ten minutes, it was empty apart from Ani, her little brother Amit, her mum and Miya.

"That's strange," Mrs Daswani said. "When I dropped you and Kit off after school yesterday, your mum said she was coming this afternoon."

Miya bit her lip and looked outside for the hundredth time.

"Let's give her a call," said Mrs Daswani.

Miya's home number was busy.

"That means she's there!" exclaimed Mrs Daswani. "It must have slipped her mind. But don't worry, we can walk you home, like normal."

Ten minutes later, they were standing on Miya's doorstep, ringing the bell.

There was the sound of running footsteps and the door was flung open.

"I'm still in a phone meeting … Oh!" said Mum, flustered. Then, looking past Miya, Ani, Amit and Mrs Daswani, she shouted, "Where are Obaachan and Kit, Miya? They went to pick you up!"

Mrs Daswani took charge. "You go back to your meeting, Eiko. The kids can stay here and I'll go look around. They can't be far."

Miya's mum clasped her friend's hand gratefully. "Thank you. She seemed so alert and with it today, I thought—"

Mrs Daswani squeezed back. "Don't worry."

Miya and Ani had barely had time to get a drink of water when the front door slammed and Kit ran in.

"We bought cake!" he shouted.

Mrs Daswani and Gran followed, chatting. Mum clattered down the stairs and rushed into the kitchen too.

"Oh, thank you, thank you, Gita. You're a gem. Where were they?" she gasped, hand on chest.

"No problem!" said Mrs Daswani. "They'd just gone to the shops."

Gran smiled apologetically. "Sorry, I forgot the time," she said as Miya's mum examined her anxiously. "Everybody relax. I'll make tea and cake."

13

"Mum, why didn't you come to pick me up today?" Miya asked that night.

Her mum sat next to her and ran her fingers around the pattern on a cushion.

"I was too busy ... I know I said I'd be less busy from this week, but someone quit at work and they asked me to cover for them," she said, not meeting Miya's eyes. "I'm sorry. I promise it won't be forever. And Ani's mum said she'll walk you back every week, so you can still go to Theatre Club."

"Why were you so angry when I got home?"

Mum sighed. "I wasn't angry, I was scared. I thought Obaachan and Kit had got lost."

Miya sat up. "How could they have got lost?" she asked.

"Well ... they weren't lost – " replied Mum. "It was my mistake. I got worried for nothing. Go to bed and don't fret, OK?"

Miya nodded, but the squirmy feeling was back, and getting harder to ignore.

Tuesday, 1st March

Really bad day

Thursday, 3rd March

Even worse day

4 Missing Toto

The sun was streaming in from the window behind Miya, drenching the battered sofa and her sketchbook in golden light.

Kit wandered in and threw himself down next to her. "I miss Daddy and Toto," he said.

Miya nodded. "Me too."

"Whatcha doing?" asked Kit, craning over to look.

Miya quickly flipped her sketchbook closed. "I'm writing my journal."

"Why?"

"It was my New Year's resolution to, but I've fallen behind."

Kit thought for a bit, then asked, "What's a journal?"

Miya rolled her eyes. "A book where I write and draw my thoughts."

"Can I see?"

Miya shook her head. "No. It's private," she snapped, adding, "that means I'm the only one allowed to look at it." She could see her brother was about to ask why again, but the phone rang and gave her a chance to escape.

"Hello?" The voice didn't sound familiar.

Miya, who'd been hoping it would be Jess or Ani, stifled a sigh.

"Hello," she replied.

"Have you lost your dog?" continued the voice.

"Yes," said Miya excitedly. "He's white and he's called Toto! Is he there? Is he OK?"

"Yes, he's fine. He's sitting next to me. I spotted him in my front garden a few days ago, eating the food I left out for the hedgehogs, but it took me ages to catch him!"

Friday, 4th March

Toto's back!

5 Making up

Miya cuddled Toto and thought about how she'd felt earlier. She'd been disappointed when she'd picked up the phone and heard a stranger's voice.

She wandered over to Gran and sat down.

"Obaachan, did you ever fight with your friends?" she asked.

Gran set her knitting aside.

"All friends fight from time to time," she said, patting Miya's knee. "What happened?"

Miya blew out a gusty sigh. "Me, Ani and Jess promised to go in matching costumes that spelt out our book title for World Book Day. But Mum didn't buy the art supplies so I couldn't."

21

"What did your friends say?"

"That I'd wrecked our plans. But it wasn't my fault!"

"Did you explain why you weren't in costume?"

Miya paused, then replied in a little voice, "No. I said the costumes were a dumb idea."

Gran pulled Miya close. "I had an argument with Sadako once," she reminisced. "We were so angry we didn't talk for five days. My big brother got sick of us being silent and cross, so he wrote an apology note to each of us, pretending it was from the other. As soon as we got the notes, we ran to apologise too, and it was only afterwards that we discovered that he'd tricked us!"

"Were you angry at him then?"

Gran shook her head. "No, we felt silly, having wasted time being angry, because we were both too proud to be the first to say sorry."

Miya thought about that, then asked, "Obaachan, can you help me call Jess and Ani's parents to ask if they can come over?"

Gran smiled. "Of course I'll help. Friends are precious!"

Saturday, 5th March

Friday, 11th March

Dad's home!

6 Pizza party fail

School had been fun on the last day before the Easter holidays … Mr Kara had given us a break from SATs revision and played an April Fool's joke on the class, then the end of term bell had rung at noon. Mum had promised to pick Miya, Jess and Ani up and take them for pizza … but when they ran into the hall at noon, Jess's mum was waiting there instead.

"There's been a little accident at Miya's house," she said.

WORDSEARCH

WORDS TO FIND:
friends
happy
laugh
good
holiday
family

First one to find all six words wins a prize!

o	p	t	a	s	n	e	s	a	u
t	e	x	p	l	i	a	m	q	u
u	n	t	i	s	s	i	n	t	s
g	e	n	s	t	c	t	e	n	i
s	t	v	e	l	i	a	n	i	m
n	e	e	t	u	t	e	t	l	m
x	i	m	r	e	m	d	o	l	u
p	t	a	c	u	s	i	o	f	f
c	i	a	n	d	u	c	i	u	s
a	l	i	q	u	i	a	e	t	a
s	e	a	s	e	q	u	a	m	c

Seeing Miya's face, she hurriedly added, "Don't worry, it's not too bad … But we have to cancel lunch for today. I'll take you all home, then we'll arrange another meet up – in a few days."

"Can they come to our place instead?" asked Jess.

Mrs Grant hesitated. "I don't mind, but I think Miya's mum needs her today," she answered.

"But we haven't hung out after school for ages!" wailed Ani.

Miya bit her lip. "You still can," she muttered.

Mrs Grant smiled at Miya. "Well, if you're sure, Miya. I can drop you home first, then take Jess and Ani back to ours. And we'll definitely arrange something for all three of you next week."

"Miya's got to come!" Jess said, tugging at her mother's arm. "Can't you call her mum and beg?"

Mrs Grant shook her head. "I already suggested it."

Ten minutes later, Miya was standing at her front gate.

"Let's J.A.M. sandwich!" said Ani. They squashed into a group hug, but all too soon, Miya was waving goodbye as her friends disappeared.

Why wouldn't Mum let me go? It just wasn't fair!

Miya flung the front door open, ready to march in and yell at her mum …

But the smell of burning and the wisps of smoke hanging in the corridor caused a cold gush of fear to put out the flames of her anger. She could hear someone weeping,

and her mother's voice, gently murmuring something. Heart pounding, she turned the corner to the lounge.

Mum was sitting on the sofa, her arms around Gran, who was slumped against the cushions, crying softly. Kit was on the rug, quiet and still for once, gazing up at Gran, with wide, worried eyes.

"What happened? Is … is Obaachan OK?" asked Miya.

Gran started crying harder.

"Miya, I didn't make it – " she sobbed.

Mum beckoned. "Oh sweetheart, come and give Obaachan a hug. She was making yakisoba, but she forgot to turn off the stove, and it caught on fire. She's hurt her hands trying to put out the flames too."

Friday, 1st April

Fire!

7 Easter holidays

Miya sighed and gazed gloomily at the chocolate rabbit
on the mantlepiece. It beamed back at her through
the cellophane on the box.

Miya wasn't happy at all. Her life and all her plans had
turned upside down. Easter break was almost over, and she
hadn't even seen her friends.

Things had been so good before the holidays …
After Toto and Dad had come home, Mum had been more
relaxed and ready to chat and smile.

Dad had brought back a cookbook from New York, and
announced that he and Miya were going to cook dinner every
day to give Gran and Mum a break.

Miya had loved cooking with Dad, though not
the cleaning up – which took ages. She'd been so busy that
she'd barely had time to draw in her journal.

Still, she hadn't minded. She hadn't even cared that
the dinners had been a bit repetitive because Dad cooked
his four favourite dishes in rotation.

But, the night before the fire, sitting down to macaroni
cheese again, Miya had leant over and whispered to Gran,
"I miss your Japanese yakisoba!"

"I'll make it for you soon!" Gran had whispered back.

Miya had gone to bed, dreaming of the yummy
fried noodles.

She wished, wished, wished she hadn't mentioned
yakisoba to Gran.

Since the fire, Gran no longer read magazines, knitted
or chatted with Miya and Kit. She just sat in her chair with
her bandaged hands in her lap, looking at the television for
hours – though she didn't seem to be actually watching.

Mum was super-stressed again, and Miya had been
put on all-day babysitting duties for Kit, who had been
very whiny. Even Dad wasn't smiling much anymore.

It was all her fault …

8 Cookie bake

Going back to school after the dull, depressing Easter break made a nice change. The classroom was buzzing with excitement.

Jess reached into her bag and brought out two paper bags. She handed one to Miya and the other to Ani.

"Mum and I baked some hot cross buns on Easter Sunday, so I brought some to share with my besties!"

Miya opened her bag and inhaled the warm scent of cinnamon and sugar. She sighed with pleasure.

"*Mmrmwah,*" said Ani, taking a bite. "Jessie, it's soooo good! Can you teach me to bake?"

Jess grinned. "Mum's teaching me to bake choc chip cookies this Wednesday. Do you two want to come?"

"Do we ever!" cheered Miya.

Later that evening, Dad made dinner. He'd decided to celebrate the kitchen being fixed, by cooking a family favourite called "om-rice" which Gran pronounced "omu-ra-issu". Miya loved how it looked like a rugby ball-shaped omelette, but when you cut into the egg, you discovered it was stuffed with a tomatoey fried rice studded with chicken, onions and peas.

"Now I tuck this omelette around the rice and flip it onto the plate, right?" asked Dad.

Gran nodded.

Miya clapped and cheered as Dad laid it on the table next to the salad.

"Dig in, everyone!" he said.

"I don't want salad," said Kit.

"No salad, no dessert!" replied Dad.

"You made dessert?" asked Mum in astonishment.

Dad laughed. "I just bought berries!" he admitted.

That reminded Miya about Jess's invitation. "I'll be able to make dessert soon," she said. "Jess's mum is teaching us how to make choc chip cookies, on Wednesday, after school."

"Oh," said Dad, and looked at his plate. Mum fell silent too. Miya's smile slipped from her face.

"I can go, right?" she asked.

Dad cleared his throat. "Actually," he said. "We need to ask you a favour ... As Mum and I are so busy with work, can you be home a bit more to keep an eye on Kit?"

"I'm sorry but that means no more after-school activities or playdates, just for a little while," added Mum.

Miya gasped. "What's a little while?" she asked.

Mum hesitated. "The person my company was hoping to hire didn't work out. I'm not sure when, but as soon we get someone, I'll go part-time, and you'll be free again."

Miya looked at Gran. "Why can't Obaachan look after Kit?" she said.

Gran, who had been gazing at her food, looked up. "What?" she asked.

Mum shook her head at Gran and replied in a gentle voice, "Don't worry. We're fine."

Miya got up and threw her napkin down. "Well, *I'm* not fine!" she shouted, then stomped out.

9 Gran's memory

Throwing herself onto the sofa, Miya fumed, halfway between anger and tears.

Every time she thought about the fire and how quiet and sad Gran had become since that day, the squirmy feeling took over and made her scared and breathless, until she squashed it into the back of her mind.

To distract herself, she'd read or drawn in her journal every day, sitting with Kit and Gran – the three of them lonely islands in a sea of silence – while Mum worked, only coming downstairs for meals. And, although she'd been bored and longing to see friends, Miya hadn't complained. Not once.

Going back to school today, had been so much fun. Miya had felt like she finally had her life back. She hadn't expected the bombshell they'd thrown at dinner.

She looked up at a knock, but she didn't smile as Dad came in. Mum stayed by the door, her arms tightly wrapped around herself.

Dad stretched out his hand to stroke Miya's hair but she flinched away.

"If I don't go to rehearsals, I'll let everyone down," she said. "Then they'll hate me."

"I promise no one will hate you, Miya. Mum called Mr Kara today. He understands, and he'll explain the situation to everyone," he said, gently.

Mum made an impatient noise. "Miya, you know Obaachan hasn't been herself since the fire. I'm working downstairs while you're at school so I can help her, but I have meetings in the afternoon, so I want your help to keep watch and call me when I'm needed. I'm sorry. It's not ideal for me either, but we all have to pitch in. And it'll give you time to study for your SATs –"

"I didn't *mean* to cause the fire," Miya interrupted, in a trembling voice.

Mum stopped speaking and looked at her in shock.

Miya buried her face in her hands and sobbed. "I told Obaachan that I missed her yakisoba. It's all my fault."

A second later, Miya was wrapped in both her parents' arms.

"Sweetheart," said Mum, her voice warm and comforting. "The fire was *not* your fault. It was no one's fault. It was just an accident."

Dad nodded. "Obaachan's memory isn't working properly anymore. Sometimes she forgets things but that's not her fault either. She's doing her best."

"She's still the same Obaachan who loves us – so we just have to love her back and look after her, like she looked after us all these years," said Mum.

Miya wiped her eyes and sat up. "I will, I promise."

Mum smiled. "Thank you."

Saturday, 23rd April

No more Knave of Hearts

Monday, 23rd May

Things I miss

10 Pity party

Miya bent over her journal, pen in hand. The library was cool and quiet. Ms Nasser, the librarian, pushed her library cart past and smiled.

"How's the project going?" she asked.

"Fine," she said, covering up the page with her sleeve.

These days she had plenty of time to write her journal, but she hadn't felt like it, until today.

As Ms Nasser turned away, Miya blurted out, "Ms Nasser, how are you always so happy?"

Ms Nasser stopped, and knelt down. "I … Are you unhappy, child?" she asked.

Miya sighed. "No – " she said slowly. "I'm OK."

Ms Nasser gazed at her intently, then said, "It's good to be happy, but it's also all right to be sad. We can't be happy all the time."

"Are you ever sad?" asked Miya.

"Of course," said Ms Nasser. "But I find that talking about it with a friend helps. We throw a pity party, do some wild dancing and laugh, then I usually feel better!"

Miya giggled at the thought of Ms Nasser, who always looked so neat and grown up, doing wild dancing.

"You should try it sometime, it's a lot of fun … especially if you have ice cream to cool you down afterwards!"

Ms Nasser winked, then got up. "If you ever need a partner for a pity party or some wild dancing, you know where to find me," she said, then left.

Miya opened her journal and reread her latest entry.

She put a neat line through her title and wrote above it:

MIYA'S PITY PARTY

She added a little picture of some balloons by the side and a little stick girl wild dancing. Ms Nasser was right – even just thinking about wild dancing made her feel more light-hearted.

Miya looked up as the doors banged open and Ani and Jess appeared.

"Miya!" shouted Jess. "Yay, found you! Rehearsals finished early, so we can do Double Dutch."

"Coming!" Miya said, gathering her things. "You get the skipping ropes."

Jess ran off, while Ani waited. "Why're you in the library?" she asked curiously.

"I – " Miya hesitated. "I was talking to Ms Nasser."

"About what?"

Miya looked into Ani's kind brown eyes. She wanted to tell her that it felt like Ani and Jess had got jetpacks, and were zooming around the stars having adventures, while she was stuck on the ground, forgotten, her feet buried deep in the mud … But when she thought of saying it out loud, she felt her breath catch. Instead she said, "About a book."

Ani smiled and linked her arm in Miya's. "Let's go. Jess will be waiting!" she said.

Miya smiled back, but she wasn't sure if she was happy or sad that Ani had believed her.

11 Dance party

Later that afternoon, when Miya and Kit got home, they found Mum and Gran in the kitchen and a sweet scent in the air.

As always, as she entered the room, Miya's eyes went to Gran. Over the last month, as the burns on her hands had healed, she'd slowly become more cheerful. Sometimes she called Miya "Sadako" and got muddled up in the middle of doing something, but Miya didn't mind so much anymore.

It was nice to have smiley, chatty Obaachan back.

"What's that smell?" said Kit, nose in the air like a bloodhound. "I'm hungry!"

Mum swung him up off the ground, grabbed Miya in her other arm, and gave them both a hug.

"I had an unexpected afternoon off," she said, beaming. "So Obaachan and I went for a walk, and we've made some cupcakes! Grab one and tell us about school."

"It was fine," said Miya. "But eating cupcakes is better."

Kit nodded, mouth full.

Gran laughed. "What did you learn today?" she asked.

"I learnt that wild dancing makes people happy," Miya answered.

Gran sighed happily. "Any dancing makes me happy," she said. "My father learnt ballroom dancing in Kobe. When I was a child, he'd put on the music, I'd stand on his feet, then he'd whirl me around!"

"I remember you telling me that when I was young!" said Mum. "Shall we put some music on?"

43

Thursday, 2nd June

Wild dancing really works!

Friday, 24th June

Maths problem

12 Meiling

Miya first set eyes on Meiling on the first Friday in July.

Just as the Maths lesson started that afternoon, the classroom door opened, and Ms Peters, their head teacher, walked in with a new girl. Her hair was in the shiniest, neatest bob Miya had ever seen.

"Class, I'd like you to welcome Meiling Tsui, who'll be joining us next Monday. Her family have just moved from Hong Kong." Ms Peters smiled at Jess who was grinning and waving to the new girl. "Meiling, I believe you know Jess?"

Meiling nodded shyly and said, "She lives next door."

Mr Kara got a chair and put it next to Jess. "Seven to a table is a bit of a squash," he said, "but it'll do for now!"

Jess introduced Meiling to everyone at the table. "This is Robin, Brian and Vijay," she said, "… this is Ani, who is my oldest friend, and this is Miya."

Miya waited for Jess to tell Meiling that she was Jess's second oldest friend, but Jess was already talking about something else.

They'd said sorry, but since last week, when Jess had accused Miya of cheating, and Miya had been mean back, things had been weird between them.

Thinking about that made Miya feel cross again … and a little guilty too.

Tapping Jess on the arm, Miya said, "We should finish off our maths … Mr Kara keeps looking over."

Jess wrinkled her nose and said to Meiling, "Miya loves Maths. Because she's *MUCH* smarter than Ani and me."

Miya got up, saying, "Mr Kara's right, seven to a table is a bit of a squash." She moved her chair over to a nearby space. She was busy holding back tears, so she didn't notice Ani frowning at Jess, and Meiling saying, "My mum's a Maths teacher, and I like Maths too."

Friday, 1st July

Meiling joins our class

13 All change

On Monday morning, Miya's class discovered their whole classroom had been shifted around.

"Surprise!" said Mr Kara. "I've mixed you all up, so you get used to sitting with and making new friends. I know that a lot of you are nervous about going to a secondary school soon which is a lot bigger, or going to different schools from your friends, so this will be good practice."

"My brother said the Year 13s are huge and scary!" shouted Brian.

Mr Kara nodded. "Yes, being new, being the smallest, being separated from your buddies, not knowing the people in your class, even getting lost is what a lot of Year Six children worry about."

Looking at their worried faces, he smiled. "We can't help you grow taller, but we're going to make sure that new environments and new people won't worry you. For these last three weeks of term, you're going to sit with some familiar faces, and less familiar faces, and practise getting to know each other!"

Everyone scattered to look for their names on the seats.

Miya was with Jess, Olivia, George, Sayed and Darius. Ani was on the next table with Meiling, Sophie, Leo, Robin and Noah.

Jess put up her hand. "Mr Kara, can I swap with Sophie?" she said. "Only, it's not fair that Ani hasn't got anyone she knows well."

Mr Kara shook his head. "Ani knows Robin," he said. "Besides, she's just on the next table, not on Mars!"

The morning passed swiftly. It was Monday, so Jess and Ani had a lunchtime rehearsal. Meiling went with them to watch.

Olivia asked Miya to play tag, which was more fun than Miya expected.

"What did you think of the table swap today?" asked Ani, as they walked home that afternoon.

"It was OK," said Miya. "Everyone is nice. Sayed is funny, and Olivia is friendly. How about you?"

"I missed you and Jess, but I really like Meiling. She's a bit shy, like you, but she's lots of fun, once you get to know her."

Monday, 4th July
OLIVIA

52

"Am I fun too?" asked Miya.

"Of course! Super fun," said Ani, as they reached Miya's home. "See you tomorrow!"

That night, Miya had a nightmare. In it, Dream Ani was telling Dream Jess that Meiling was shy but fun like Miya.

Dream Jess said, "We don't need Miya anymore. She's always busy and thinks she's smarter than us."

"But I'd miss our J.A.M. sandwiches!" said Dream Ani, talking about their group hugs.

"Meiling starts with M, so we can do J.A.M. sandwiches with her instead," said Dream Jess.

Miya woke up, with a gasp. How would she cope if her best friends abandoned her? She didn't sleep again that night.

14 Alice in Wonderland

The Theatre Club play was wonderful.

Miya cheered and clapped as it ended, although she felt a little sad that she wasn't on the stage too.

Right after the show there was a party outside. Miya and her family met up with Ani, Jess and their families.

"You were fantastic," said Miya, giving Jess and Ani a shy smile.

"Yes, it was wonderful," said Gran. "I wish I could sing like that again!"

"Were you a performer in the past?" asked Ani's dad.

"I used to sing every Sunday with my sister and brother, for our parents," said Gran wistfully.

"I didn't know that!" said Mum, in surprise. "We should do little shows at home too."

"I'll dust off my guitar!" said Dad.

Jess's mum turned as Meiling's family approached.

"Hello!" she said. "Everyone, have you met our new neighbours, Samson and Rosa Tsui and their daughter Meiling?"

Meiling pulled Jess and Ani into a group hug. "Congrats! You were SOOOOO good!" she said. Then, turning to Miya, "We should join too, in Year Seven!"

Miya, who'd been feeling left out, nodded and crossed her fingers. She felt a gush of relief and joy when Jess and Ani smiled and crossed their fingers too.

Friday, 22nd July
OBAACHAN THE STAR!

15 End of term

The last week of term had been a whirlwind, but it had been all right. Jess had been chattier, and Miya had grown closer to Olivia and Sayed.

Miya couldn't believe her primary school days were over.

"Tonight was fun, wasn't it?" Mum asked, coming in.

Miya nodded. "Obaachan was really good!"

"Yes!" Mum laughed.

"Mum, how come she can remember singing as a kid, but forget the play last week?"

"It's odd how memory works," mused Mum. "Sometimes as we get older, it gets harder for new memories to stick … but the older memories seem to stay in our minds for longer and become easier to remember than what happened yesterday."

"That's sad. Will she get better?"

Mum put an arm around Miya. "I'm afraid not," she said. "I'm really sad too, because she may become even more forgetful than this. But we'll face those worries when they come. For now, let's appreciate the good things, like her stories about her childhood. I haven't heard some of them before and they're so interesting!"

"Maybe I can draw some illustrations for them."

"She'd love that … and I would too," said Mum. "Thank you, dear."

16 Summer holidays

Miya looked up as Mum clattered down the stairs.

"Can't believe it's lunchtime already," Mum said, bustling around making sandwiches. "What have you lot been up to?"

"Kit and Obaachan have been working on a colouring book together. Earlier, Obaachan told us about the picnics Sadako and her used to have under the cherry blossoms in spring, so I drew a picture of that," said Miya showing the picture.

Mum went misty-eyed. "That's lovely," she said. "It's called hanami. I did that when I was young too. You get showered with pink petals every time the breeze blows."

"Mummy, I'm booored – " moaned Kit over lunch. "I want to go to the park!"

Miya had promised to keep Kit busy while Mum worked, but it was only the first Monday of August – less than two weeks since the end of term – and they were already annoying each other.

Mum looked at her watch. "I'm sorry but I have meetings all afternoon," she told Kit.

"Obaachan can take us!" wailed Kit.

Mum looked doubtful. "Why don't we all go for a walk later?" she said.

Kit threw himself on the floor and kicked his feet. Miya rolled her eyes. It was going to be a long afternoon.

Friday evening took forever to arrive. Miya had been counting the days since Dad had suggested they invite Jess and Ani for a DIY pizza night. She'd almost asked Dad if she could invite Meiling, but Kit had wanted Amit to come, so she'd kept quiet.

She was glad she hadn't invited her, once her friends arrived.

As they rolled out the pizza dough Dad had prepared, Ani and Jess talked endlessly about what they'd been doing with Meiling while Miya had been at home with Gran and Kit.

Meiling had got a trampoline which they'd been practising on … Meiling's parents had taken them to their sports club for swimming lessons … Meiling had got a dog they'd been helping to train.

And then, worst of all – Meiling's family were taking the three girls to the seaside for the whole of the following week.

"But – " said Miya, "but next Wednesday is the tenth – "

Ani gasped. "Oh, it's your birthday!" She looked at Jess in dismay. "What should we do?"

"Maybe we could ask Meiling if Miya could come?" said Jess hesitantly.

Miya, who'd been hoping they'd decide not to go, shook her head. "The seaside's boring," she said firmly. "I've got more interesting plans!"

17 Turning 11

"Happy Birthday, Miya!"

"Thanks."

"We wish you were here. Are you having fun?"

"Yes, tons! So busy, I have to go, BYE!"

Miya put down the phone, cutting off Jess, Ani and Meiling. She wondered if she'd made a mistake, insisting that she didn't want to go, when Meiling's parents had rung hers to invite her to the seaside.

As it was Miya's birthday, Ani's mum had picked up Kit for a playdate with Amit, so that Miya, Mum and Gran could go out for a special birthday lunch.

Only … just as they were about to leave, Miya's mum had got a call from work about an emergency, and she'd gone upstairs, saying, "I'll just be a minute."

Miya smoothed out her new outfit and looked at the clock again. She and Gran had been waiting so long, Gran had dozed off. She hoped that being 11 was going to get better.

Wednesday, 10th August

11th birthday

18 Year Seven

Two weeks before the new school year, a letter had arrived telling Miya she was in Class 7W at Harlow House Secondary. She wondered which class Jess and Ani were in.

During previous summers, she'd seen them almost every day, but not this year. They'd seen each other once for Miya's delayed birthday party, to which she'd invited Olivia, Jess and Ani, Sayed, George and Darius, but not since.

Mum came in humming. She'd finally gone back to part-time work and was much more relaxed. "Why don't you invite your friends over?" she asked.

"Don't feel like it," Miya muttered.

"They've called you so many times, but you never go. What's wrong?"

"Nothing."

Starting at the new school was scary. It was so big and noisy. Miya was hoping to see Ani or Jess when she walked into 7W on the first day, but there was only Meiling, waving. She pretended not to see her, but Meiling ran up and hugged her.

"Miya!" she said. "I'm so glad you're in my class. I've saved you the seat next to me!"

Miya sat down grumpily as Meiling chatted. "Did you have a good summer? I wish you could've come to the seaside. We missed you."

Miya spent break and lunchtime with Ani and Jess, who were in Class 7F, but it wasn't the same with Meiling there.

She didn't say much – and didn't see the worried looks the other three gave her.

65

"It's so unfair." Miya stamped her feet, making Kit laugh. She glared at him. "Mum, I haven't got either Ani or Jess in my class. I don't even have Olivia."

Mum gave Miya a sympathetic look. "Meiling is there, though – "

"I don't even like her!" Miya said, bursting into tears.

Miya felt Gran's gentle hand on hers.

"Don't be sad, Sadako. What's wrong?" she asked.

Miya leapt up. "I'm NOT Sadako! I'm MIYA … MIYA!" she shouted, then ran out.

She heard Gran saying in a shaky voice, "What's happening?" and Mum answering, but Miya didn't stop moving until she was in bed buried under her duvet.

The next day was no better. Meiling wouldn't stop chatting and smiling at Miya, or looking anxiously at her when she thought Miya wasn't looking.

At lunchtime, Miya hid in the library, behind some shelves, so she wouldn't have to talk to anyone.

Then, when she got home, she discovered that Mum had arranged a tea party. "Surprise! Ani, Jess and Meiling are coming soon!" Mum said. "Obaachan and I baked a cake."

"I don't want to see them," said Miya. As she rushed out, she bumped into Gran. A trayful of mugs crashed to the floor.

"Look what you've done! You've broken my favourite mug!" yelled Miya.

Gran gasped. "I'm sorry, Sadako – "

"I'M MIYA, can't you remember anything?!" Miya screamed.

67

19 Mood change

The atmosphere at dinner that night was awful. Both Mum and Miya were grumpy. Gran was really down.

"What happened? Why are you so sad?" Dad asked Gran.

Gran gave him a wobbly smile. "I … can't remember … I'm fine," she said.

Miya felt her chest tighten. She'd planned to apologise to Gran for upsetting her, but if she'd forgotten why she was sad, should she remind her?

Instead, she went over and wrapped Gran in a bear hug. "I love you SOOO very much, Obaachan," she said, smiling at her.

A smile spread across Gran's face, until she was lit up with happiness.

She cuddled Miya back. "I love you too!"

Sunday, 11th September

What I learnt from Obaachan

Friends are precious!

Don't wait to say
  you're sorry.

Tell people
  what's happening.

Wild dancing rules!

Always try your
very best – sing like
  you're a superstar!

Be kind and caring!

When someone's sad, they stay sad,
even when they can't remember why,
  so make them happy.

Loving someone is
more important than
remembering their name.

Smile, 'cos smiles
are contagious!

Miya felt happier the following Monday. She reread her latest journal entry when she got to school, and decided to follow Gran's wisdom. She even smiled at Meiling, before going to help the teacher carry some books.

Her good mood vanished though, when she saw Meiling reading the page she'd left her journal open at.

How dare she? Miya thought, running across the classroom. *That's private!*

But the words died in her throat when she noticed Meiling wiping her eyes.

"Miya, you're such a good artist," she said. "I miss my grandma in Hong Kong so much. Ani and Jess told me about your Gran. I was looking forward to meeting her and I was sad when tea was cancelled. I hope she feels OK today."

Shame flushed Miya's cheeks red.

"She's OK," she said. Then, in a rush, confessed, "I upset her and everyone, by shouting. That's why tea was cancelled. I'm sorry."

"You must have been upset too," Meiling said sympathetically. "What happened?"

The whole story tumbled out of Miya. How Gran couldn't remember things anymore. How she'd had to quit Theatre Club and stay home a lot because Mum and Dad had been too busy to mind Kit, and Gran no longer could.

"That sounds tough," said Meiling, adding, "You should tell the others. We thought you didn't want to hang out because you hated me."

"I don't hate you," said Miya, realising that this was true. "But I was jealous of you. I thought Ani and Jess liked you more than me."

Meiling laughed. "What? No way! They've been really worried about you. You're their bestie!"

Even so, Miya felt hot and cold when she joined the others at lunchtime. She needn't have worried. As soon as she appeared, Jess and Ani yelled, "MIYA!" and pulled her into a group hug.

"Meiling, you too!" said Miya. "Let's have a J.A.M.M. sandwich hug, then we need to talk!"

That evening, Miya confided to her parents too, about how frustrated and lonely she'd been feeling at home and school.

"I'm sorry we didn't speak sooner," said Mum, tenderly. "We've also been feeling sad and frustrated, but we didn't want you to worry."

Dad nodded. "You're not alone. We'll get through it together."

A few days later, they had a tea party.

"Obaachan, meet my new friend, Meiling!" said Miya. "And, do you remember my friends, Ani and Jess?"

"I think so!" giggled Gran.

That afternoon Gran told stories about her childhood, and heard many stories in return. She sometimes got muddled about who was who, but she enjoyed the stories anyway when Mum explained, showed her pictures and filled in the details.

Watching her, Miya realised that getting a story straight didn't matter. It was being with people who loved and cared for her, that made Gran happy. *That* was the most important thing.

20 Birthday surprise

Miya pulled her friends into the kitchen.

"For Gran's birthday, I want to make something special to remind us of all the people and stories she loves. Then, we'll always be able to talk about them with her."

"Like … a family tree with stories?!" asked Meiling.

"Exactly!" said Miya.

"You can use the drawings you did of her stories – like the cherry blossom one!" suggested Ani.

"Great idea, I've got loads!" said Miya.

"It's gotta be big!" added Jess.

Mum who was walking by, commented, "You could paint it on the wall!"

Miya grinned. "I'll need some help!"

"Try and stop us!" said Jess.

Miya wiped away a tear. "Love you guys! J.A.M.M. hug?"

Thursday, 13th October

Building Obaachan's Tree

Collecting photos

Sending Gran and Mum for a spa weekend!

Painting!

Filling the tree with people

Filling the tree with memories

21 The big day

"Shhhh!" Dad whispered as they heard the car door slam, and Mum's voice outside. Everyone listened quietly as Gran and Mum came in.

"Anyone home?" said Gran.

"SURPRISE!!"

Gran laughed delightedly, as everyone poured into the hall to wish her happy birthday.

"I forgot it was my birthday!" she said, reading the "Birthday Girl" badge someone had pinned onto her top.

Miya waited until everyone had greeted Gran.

"Happy birthday, Obaachan," she said. "May I show you your present?"

At Gran's nod, Miya took her hand and led her into the lounge.

Gran's eyes grew wide. "Oh!" she said. "Oh – " She whispered little words of delight as she walked along the tree that stretched across the wall. She studied the people, the photos and the drawings, murmuring again and again, "Oh, I recognise this!" and "So beautiful!"

"It's to help us all remember," said Miya.

"A Remember Tree – " Gran said. She touched the photo of Miya on the tree and read the label. "Look, here you are! Thank you, dearest … Miya."

How Miya feels

scared

proud

jealous

sad/lonely

angry

joyful

loving

creative

carefree

excited

bored

Ideas for reading

Written by Christine Whitney
Primary Literacy Consultant

Reading objectives:
- ask questions to improve their understanding
- predict what might happen from details stated and implied
- draw inferences such as inferring characters' feelings, thoughts and motives from their actions, and justifying inferences with evidence
- discuss their understanding and explore the meaning of words in context
- summarise the main ideas drawn from more than one paragraph, identifying key details that support the main ideas

Spoken language objectives:
- participate in discussion
- speculate, hypothesise, imagine and explore ideas through talk
- ask relevant questions

Curriculum links: Science: Animals, including humans: recognise the impact of diet, exercise, drugs and lifestyle on the way bodies function

Interest words: resolution, whirlwind, abandoned

Build a context for reading
- Look at the front cover – the illustration and the title. Encourage children to share their understanding of what the book will be about. Ask them to suggest why *My Name is Miya* appears to be stuck onto the cover of something.
- Read the blurb on the back cover. Ask children to suggest what *whirlwind of uncertainty* means.

Understand and apply reading strategies
- Read the first three chapters together. Ask children to summarise what has happened in Miya's family between 1st January and 3rd March.
- Continue to read together up to the end of Chapter 7. Ask children to explain why Miya believes *it was all her fault*.
- Read on to the end of Chapter 11. Ask children to explain what good things and what bad things happen to Miya during this time.